Ladybird Readers

Cars

Series Editor: Sorrel Pitts
Text adapted by Sorrel Pitts
Illustrated by Jenna Riggs
Song lyrics by Pippa Mayfield

LADYBIRD BOOKS

UK | USA | Canada | Ireland | Australia
India | New Zealand | South Africa

Ladybird Books is part of the Penguin Random House group of companies
whose addresses can be found at global.penguinrandomhouse.com.
www.penguin.co.uk   www.puffin.co.uk   www.ladybird.co.uk

Penguin
Random House
UK

First published 2017
Updated version reprinted 2024
006

Printed in China

The authorized representative in the EEA is Penguin Random House Ireland,
Morrison Chambers, 32 Nassau Street, Dublin D02 YH68

A CIP catalogue record for this book is available from the British Library

ISBN: 978-0-241-28354-7

All correspondence to:
Ladybird Books
Penguin Random House Children's
One Embassy Gardens, 8 Viaduct Gardens, London SW11 7BW

MIX
Paper | Supporting
responsible forestry
FSC® C018179
FSC
www.fsc.org

Ladybird Readers

Cars

Contents

Picture words

old car

family car

gas car

special car

fast car

electric car

racing car

racing driver

I love cars!

There are lots of cars.

I am a racing driver. I love driving! I drive fast cars.

Old cars

These cars are very old.

Big cars

Some cars are very big.

Do you like big cars?

big car

This is a very big car!

Small cars

These cars are very small!

small car

This is a car for one person.

Family cars

Has your family got a car?

Is it big or small?

Do you like your car?

family car

Special cars

Some special cars can drive in water or on snow.

snow

Gas and electric cars

Drivers put gas in
many cars.

gas car

These cars do not have gas.
They are electric cars.

electric car

This is an
electric car!

Fast cars

There are some very fast cars here!

Do you like fast cars?

fast car

Racing cars

Racing drivers drive these very fast cars.

racing car

I like these racing cars!

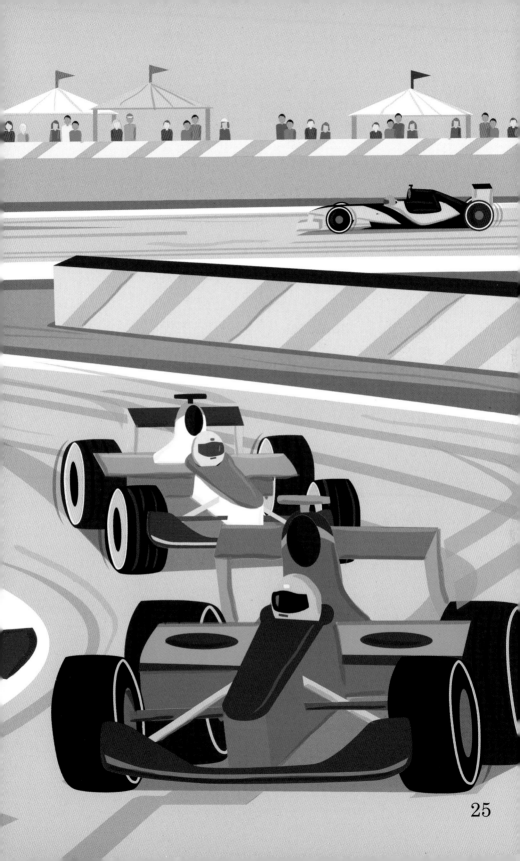

Activities

The key below describes the skills practiced in each activity.

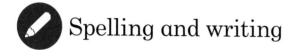 Spelling and writing

Reading

Speaking

Listening*

Critical thinking

Singing*

Preparation for the Cambridge Young Learners exams

*To complete these activities, listen to the audio downloads available at **www.ladybirdeducation.co.uk**

1 Look and read. Put a ✓ or a ✗ in the boxes. 📖 🌑

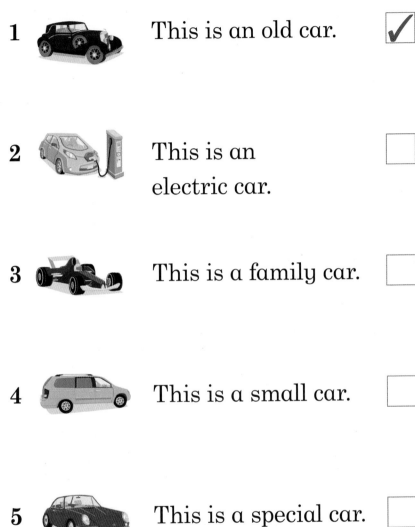

1		This is an old car.	✓
2		This is an electric car.	☐
3		This is a family car.	☐
4		This is a small car.	☐
5		This is a special car.	☐

2 Look and read. Write *yes* or *no*.

1 The racing car is fast.   ....yes...

2 The electric car is green.   ....

3 The family car is white.   ....

4 The old car is blue.   ....

5 The special car is small.   ....

3 **Work with a friend.**
Talk about the picture. ⬤ ⬤

1 How many cars can you see?

I can see three cars.

2 Where is the orange car?

It is . . .

3 Where is the boy?

He is . . .

4 Circle the correct sentences.

1
a This car is very long.
b This car is not very long.

2
a This is a special car.
b This is a racing car.

3
a These cars are not fast.
b These cars are fast!

4
a The blue car is next to the yellow car.
b The red car is next to the yellow car.

5 **Look and read. Write *these, this, These or This*.**

1 "I love _____ these _____ old cars!" says the racing driver.

2 "_____ is a very big car."

3 "_____ cars are very small."

4 "_____ driver has got an orange car."

5 "I like _____ racing car!"

6 **Read the questions.**
Write the answers. 📖 ✏️

1 Are these cars very small?

Yes, they are.

2 Is there a man in the blue car?

3 Are there children in the black car?

4 Is there a dog in the red car?

7 Circle the correct words.

1 This man and woman have
two / **three** children.

2 They have got a **racing** / **family** car.

3 Their car is **big.** / **small.**

4 Has your **fast** / **family** got a car?

8 Do the crossword.

Down

1 A ... car is very fast.

2 An ... car is not new.

4 A ... car is not slow.

Across

3 Your mom or dad drives a ... car.

5 This car is not electric. You put ... in it.

9 **Complete the sentences.**
Write a—d. 📖

1 The white car is driving ....c........

2 Some special cars ....

3 Can your car ....

4 The yellow car is ....

a very big.

b drive in water?

c in water.

d can drive on snow.

10 Find the words.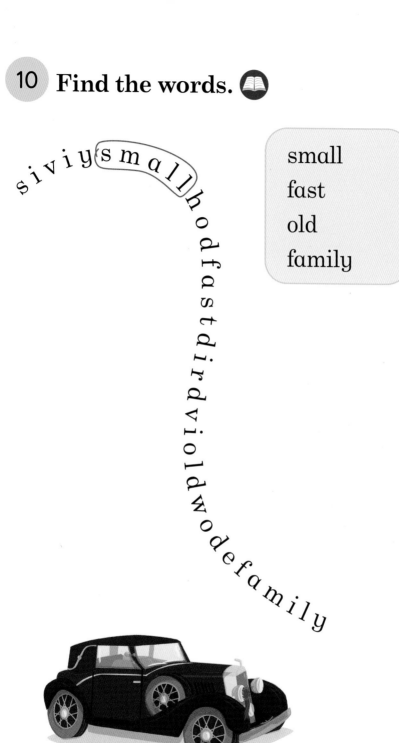

siviy(small)hodfastdirdvioldwodefamily

small
fast
old
family

11 Circle the correct pictures.

1 Which car does not have gas?

2 Which car have the mom and dad got?

3 Which car is not new?

4 Which car is good in winter?

12 **Write the correct questions.**

1 (is) (Where) (driver) (the) (?)

Where is the driver?

2 (car) (your) (Is) (this) (?)

....

3 (like) (Do) (cars) (you) (?)

....

4 (car) (Have) (got) (you) (a) (?)

....

5 (is) (car) (Which) (fast) (?)

....

13 Write the missing letters.

el	il	iv	ec	ac

1  e l ectric car

2  fam_____y car

3  r_____ing car

4  sp_____ial car

5  racing dr_____er

14 **Look at the picture and read the questions. Write one-word answers.** 📖 ✏️ ⭐

1 What is the woman with blue glasses doing?

She is ____driving____.

2 Who is wearing a red hat?

The _____ driver.

3 How many people can you see?

I can see _____ people.

15 **Ask and answer the questions with a friend.** 🗨 🗨

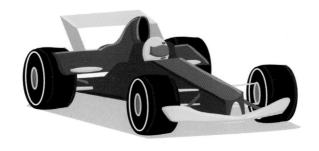

1 *What do racing drivers do?*

They drive very fast cars.

2 Do you like racing cars?

3 Has your family got an electric car?

4 Do you like your car?

16 **Match the words to the pictures.**

1 special car

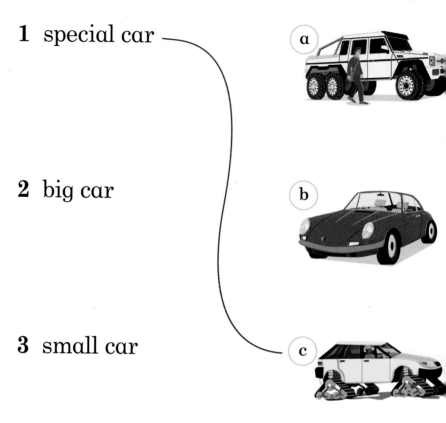

a

2 big car

b

3 small car

c

4 fast car

d

17 Write *is*, *are*, *Is* or *Are*. 📖 ✏️

1 This _____is_____ a very big car.

2 These cars _____ very old.

3 Has your family got a car? _____ it big or small?

4 _____ the racing cars fast?

5 He _____ a racing driver.

18 **Read the sentences and match them with the correct picture. Write 1—4.**

1 I am a racing driver. I love driving!

2 This driver puts gas in her car.

3 This driver has got an electric car.

4 Racing drivers drive these very fast cars.

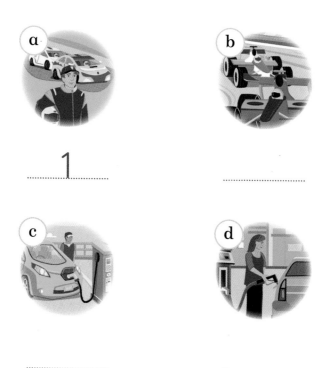

a

b

_1_

c

d

Listen, and write the answers.

1 What does he love?

_____cars_____

2 Is this car big?

_____

3 Do these cars have gas?

_____

4 Does he love racing cars?

_____

5 Are the cars big?

_____

20 Listen and color.
Use the colors below.

21 Sing the song. 🎵

Cars, cars. Brrm, brrm, brrm!
I love cars. Brrm, brrm, brrm!
Look! I am driving! Brrm, brrm, brrm!
I love cars. Brrm, brrm, brrm!

I love fast cars. I love old cars.
Cars, cars. I love cars.
I love big cars. I love small cars.
Cars, cars. I love cars.

I love driving electric cars. Sssh! Sssh!
I love driving on snow. Crunch! Crunch!
I love driving in water. Sploosh! Sploosh!
I love driving fast cars. Brrm, brrm, brrm!

Cars, cars. Brrm, brrm, brrm!
I love cars. Brrm, brrm, brrm!
Look! I am driving! Brrm, brrm, brrm!
I love cars. Brrm, brrm, brrm!

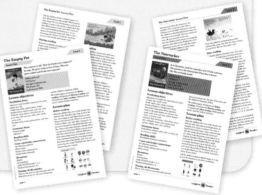